This book belongs to

Library of Congress Cataloging in Publication Data
Hall, Nancy Christensen.
Macmillan fairy tale alphabet book.
Includes index.
Summary: Presents words for each letter of the alphabet
against a background of pictures from children's "lore."
1. English language—Alphabet—Juvenile literature.
[1. Alphabet. 2. Vocabulary] I. O'Brien, John, 1953- ill.
II. Title. III. Title: Fairy tale alphabet book.
PE1155.H34   1983   [E]   82-20905
ISBN 0-02-741960-6

Macmillan
Fairy Tale
Alphabet Book

Words by Nancy Christensen Hall
Pictures by John O'Brien

Macmillan Publishing Co., Inc.
New York
Collier Macmillan Publishers
London

Copyright © 1983 Macmillan Publishing Co., Inc.
Copyright © 1983 John O'Brien
All rights reserved.
Macmillan Publishing Co., Inc.
866 Third Avenue, New York, N.Y. 10022
Collier Macmillan Canada, Inc.
Printed in the United States of America

10   9   8   7   6   5   4   3   2   1

admiring attendants

audience

amusing activity

Scheherazade's adventures held her
audiences attentive for one thousand
and one Arabian nights.

arch

amazing architecture

alike

All who approached Aladdin's
abode were awed by the affluence.

azaleas

Ali Baba

armed assassins

Ali Baba was amazed at the abundance of wealth amassed by the awful assassins.

able aide

abundance

Aladdin

adorable aristocrat

Sing a song of sixpence,
A pocket full of rye,
Four and twenty blackbirds
Baked in a pie.

blackbirds baked beard

broken bridge builders

To London

Hark, hark, the dogs do bark!
The beggars are coming to town.

barking beasts

barrel

bucket beggars

b

B

As the giant befriended the boys and girls, the blossoms began to bloom.

begonias

basket

beloved book

bugle

bass

banjo

bassoon

bouncing ball

butterflies

brave boy

beanstalk

bluebirds

bungalow

clouds

cottage

country cousin

cabbage

carrot

corn

cauliflower

celery

So the little Country Cousin went home and consumed carrots and cabbage in comfort for the rest of her days.

candle

consommé

cheese

cooked chicken

candy cane

chocolates

checkered cloth

cap

cage

canary

coffee cups

cupboard

chipped china

chair

calico

cherries

cat

city cousin

cake

claws

CIDER

The dos and don'ts of does, dogs, donkeys, and dolphins.

doe

deadly danger

daylight

dinghy

disgusted

daring dog

daffodils

doorway

damaged dishes

destroyed

dishonest

dagger

dumb dog

dinner

E

empty
entrance

English
educator

enormous

exit

envious

eggplant

elders

entertainer

eager
elves
eloping

eggs

In the times of ancient England, when elves and fairies were everyday words, the forests were enchanted.

e

F

f

flying

fun

foliage

fancy

flute

foolish
fisherman

fuel

flame

fortune

fruit

fillet of
flounder

fat

frowning

fairies feasting
on fine food

The frightened little folks fastened his hands and feet.

fortress

fleet

flagship

fastened feet

fighters

fabulous freak

fearful folk

fantastic family

flabbergasted farmer

forty-foot friend

frightened foreigner

female

fork

The farmer and his family were of fantastic size.

gigantic Gulliver

gaping

guards

ghastly

grimy

grotesque

gruesome

gentle governor

gorgeous garden

Gulliver grew fond of the gracious galloping guides.

G

grove

gingerbread

giant
gumdrops

gourds

gate

green
grass

Gretel

greedy girl

g

house

hungry
hero

horrible
hag

hearty helping

hat

heather

holly

Hansel

hummingbird

hedge

How happy they were when they first beheld
the house of the horrible hag.

heavens

highlands

hills

humble
home

high
hat

hibernating
hen-pecked
husband

half-mast

Hudson

heavy
hammer

Henry

hive

hoof

In horror they hid from the hairy
hermit when they heard
he had come home.

With hatchet in hand,
he and Babe headed for the hills.

huge hulking
hero

horns

hatchet

headless
horseman

harvest

APPLE
SEEDS

horrified
horse

hound

haunted
highway

hurrying
hare

h

island
inhabitant

icing

improper
individual

inquisitive
infant

ivory

inside

insects

ill-
humored

J

jackknife   jeans   jungle

jammed jaw

juvenile jaguar

jolly jokers

Joyful jabs at jungle creatures
for jolly little juveniles.

J

jolly jesters

joust judges

jealous joker

jug

jovial juggler

jab

junk

kingdom

kissing kin

kind king

knotting kerchief

knight kneeling

One knight knocked another
while a third knight
knelt on one knee.

The loyal little laborers
were lacing the leather.

By the light of the lamp they looked at the loads of loot.

lamplight

loot

looking

Luckily, the lovely lady liked the lion.

larks

lilacs

lion

lawn

lovely lady

moon

When old Mother Goose
Loved to roam and meander,
She'd ride to the moon
On her magical gander.

mouse

Mother
Hubbard

macaroni

MEAT MARKET

Miss Muffet

mush

mushrooms

maiden

mountains

man

mile

music

mulberry

merriment

Mary

marigolds

m

napping

nightgown

night

nestled

noble

nimble

At nighttime the nutcracker looked
noticeably like the nephew Nathaniel.

opera

overture

Orson

obnoxious offspring

ornate

Orville

overalls

overcoat

obese

onions

oranges

The ornery old lady was outnumbered by an outrageous number of offspring occupying her shoe.

ovals

owl

ocean

outhouse

oak

obscure
oysters

Olivia

Omar

Oscar

octet
of
oboists

outnumbered

opossums

P

The poor, persecuted child polished the pantry floor.

plates

pitcher

pantry

patches

pail

polishing

protector

pink plumes

pigtail

priceless pumpkin

pretty

pink petticoat

The prince pursued the person transported by pumpkin ...

The pampered pair prepared for the party.

parlor

pearls

pompous

pedestal

pageant

page

procession

...promising perpetual peace and prosperity.

"If she is a princess, she will perceive the pea," predicted the prince's parent as she planted it under the pile.

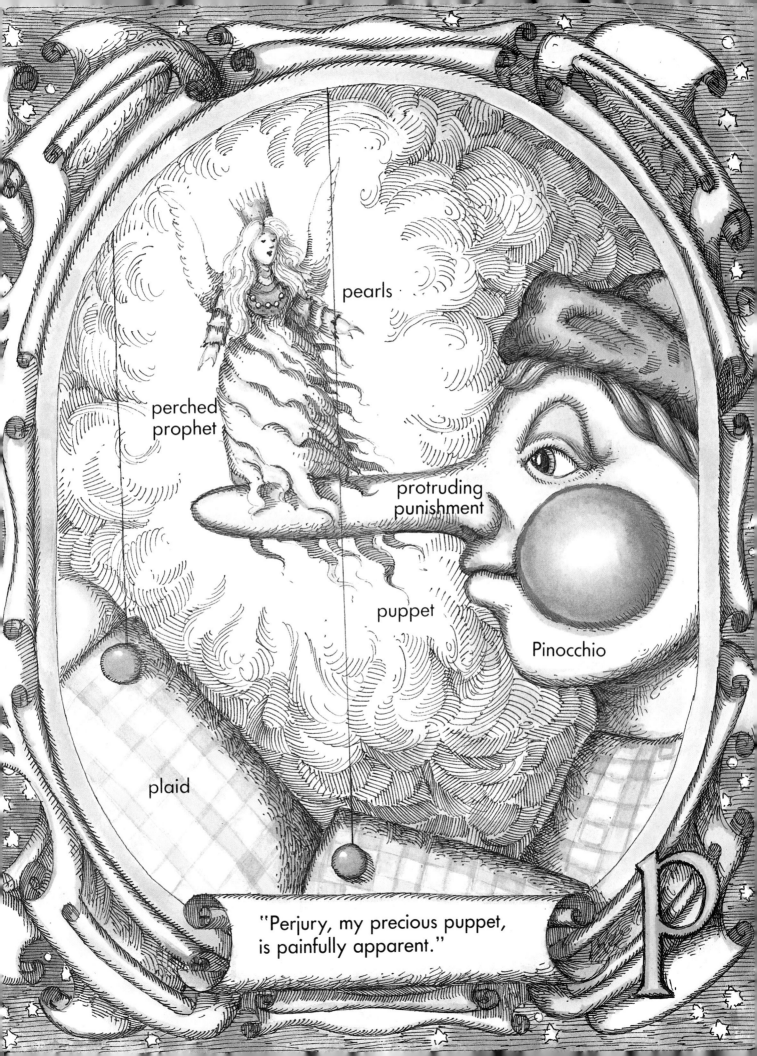

pearls

perched
prophet

protruding
punishment

puppet

Pinocchio

plaid

P

"Perjury, my precious puppet,
is painfully apparent."

relaxing on rim

ribbons

remnants

rebels
riding

ridiculous
rendezvous

roses

radiant riches

regal

royal rattle

Rumpelstiltskin

The rumor of the rapturous ravings of the ruthless Rumpelstiltskin resulted in the ruination of the wretch.

Snow White slipped soundly
into slumber
as the seven dwarfs
silently surrounded her.

shutter

shelf

sad

somber

satin
sheet

sleeping
Snow White

stricken

sorrowful

sentimental
scene

The soup was started with but a stone, then seasoned with salt and several spices...

sole

string beans

summer squash

spinach salad

sausages

shellfish

spaghetti

sugar

serving spoon

sandwiches

silverware

seat

strawberries

shut shutter

sniffing
soup

stone

salt

stirring soup

soda

sumptuous
stew

sticks

standing on
stool

S

Thumbelina

tall tulips

thin thistles

Once upon a time
there was a teeny-tiny woman,
who lived in a teeny-tiny house
in a teeny-tiny village.
One day the teeny-tiny woman
put on her teeny-tiny bonnet,
and went out of her teeny-tiny house
to take a teeny-tiny walk.

tree trunk

Tom Thumb

teeny-tiny woman

teeny-tiny tame turtle

twig

towering
toadstools

tired toad

teeny-tiny town

teeny-tiny
tombstones

teeny-tiny
house

trodden
trail

teeny-tiny
basket

teeny-tiny
rooftop

Tweedledum and Tweedledee
agreed to have a battle;
for Tweedledum said Tweedledee
had spoiled his nice new rattle.

tremendously tall

tart trial

throned tyrants

twelve

thief

teatime

top hat

teapot

toast

tired

teacup

teaspoon

table

teary turtle

torrent of tears

tiny titmouse

t

unmerciful

ugly

unusually
unpopular

Unfortunately, the Ugly Duckling was ungainly and unloved.

unfriendly

uppity

uniform

unafraid

The heart of the unsteady little soldier remained undaunted until the end.

Above the village in the valley, the vicious villain and various wretches wended their way down the winding road.

vapor

vines

vampires

venomous viper

vultures

valley

veiled villain

village

witches

winding way

woods

wretched
wife

warlock

wiggling
worms

watchful
werewolves

window

winsome
wench

watchtower
with
whitewashed
walls

wistful
wooer

warty
witch

The wretched witch kept the winsome
wench in the tower.

winter winds

worthless walls

wicked wolf

wheelbarrow

The three little pigs whistled with glee
since the wicked wolf's wind
was too weak to wreck the walls.

wolf with wig

wood

weird wardrobe

wooded walk

The wolf waited for the little waif
who was wandering through the woods.

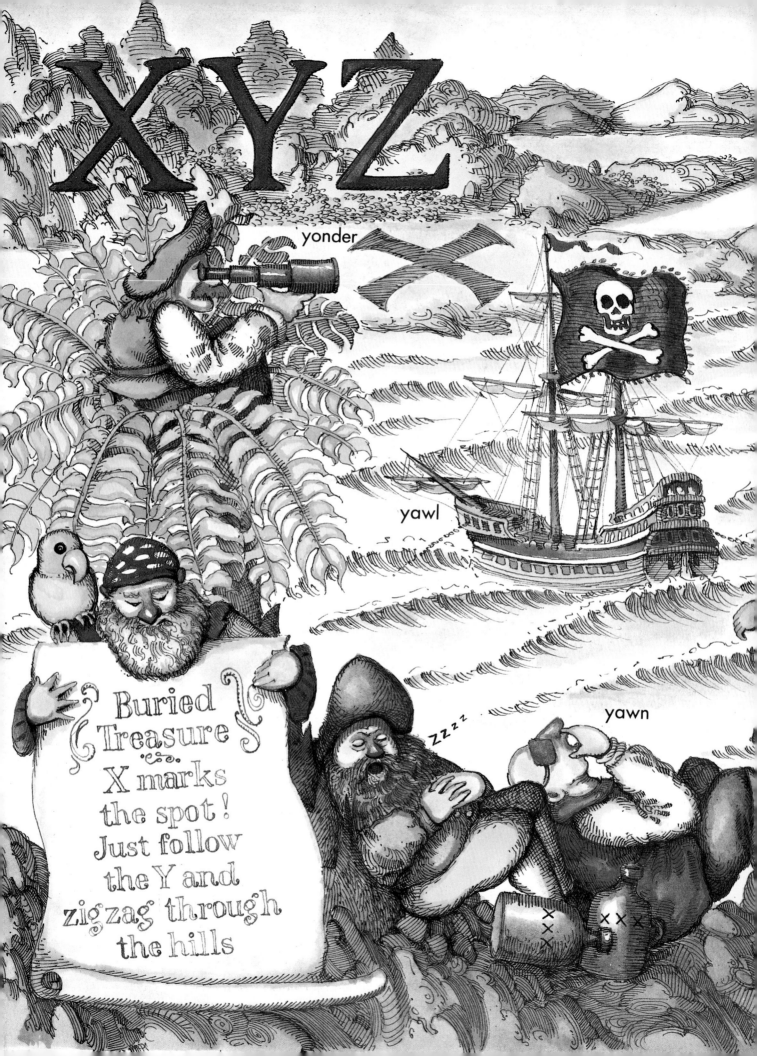

yellow

zeal

"And all the old romance, retold
Exactly in the ancient way,
Can please, as me they pleased of old,
The wiser youngsters of today."

XYZ

Key to Illustrations

 A *Arabian Nights*

Scheherazade   *The Story of Ali Baba and the Forty Thieves*
The Story of Aladdin; or, The Wonderful Lamp

B *Mother Goose Rhymes*

Fiddle-de-dee, fiddle-de-dee   *Sing a Song of Sixpence*
Little Boy Blue   *Little Bo Peep*   *Baa, Baa, Black Sheep*
Hark, Hark, the Dogs Do Bark   *London Bridge*

 B **Three Giant Stories**

The Selfish Giant   *Jack and the Beanstalk*   *Fin McCoul*

C *The Country Mouse and the City Mouse*

D *Aesop's Fables*

The One-Eyed Doe   *The Monkey and the Dolphin*
The Dog and the Manger   *The Ass and the Lap Dog*   *The Gardener and His Dog*
The Thief and the Dog   *The Ass and His Driver*

E/F **An Enchanted Forest**

 F/G *Gulliver's Travels*

A Voyage to Lilliput   *A Voyage to Brobdingnag*
Voyages to Laputa and the Country of the Houyhnhnms

G/H *Hansel and Gretel*

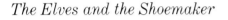

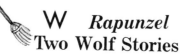